PADDINGTON™ 2

Movie Sticker Activity Book

Join Paddington for more adventures in this fantastic activity book. It's jam-packed with games, puzzles, stickers and photographs from the Paddington 2 movie.

HarperCollins PUBLISHERS

1 3 5 7 9 10 8 6 4 2

ISBN: 978-0-00-825445-2

First published by HarperCollins Children's Books in 2017

www.harpercollins.co.uk

Written by Emma Drage, designed by Claire Yeo

Welcome to Windsor Gardens!

Since Paddington moved to London, he's lived with the Brown family at 32 Windsor Gardens. Paddington is very happy in his new home!

Use your stickers to add Paddington and the Brown family to the scene.

Who else lives at Windsor Gardens?

Meet Paddington's new friends and neighbours!

Mrs Kitts runs the newspaper kiosk with her parrot, Feathers.

Mr Curry is Paddington's nosy neighbour. He thinks bears spell trouble and doesn't approve of Paddington at all!

Phoenix Buchanan used to be a very famous actor, but now he makes advertisements for dog food!

Dr Jafri likes Paddington because he always helps him when he forgets his keys!

Use your stickers to complete the photo album.

Jonathan's new look

Jonathan wants to fit in with his new friends at big school. Can you design him a cool new t-shirt?

Make a splash!

Mrs Brown is training to swim the channel. Can you design a swimsuit for her?

Use your stickers for extra decoration.

Find the keys!

Dr Jafri has forgotten his keys again! Can you find your way through the maze to help him get them back?

Start

Finish

Nosy neighbour

Mr Curry likes to keep a very close eye on all the comings and goings in Windsor Gardens. Can you spot five differences between scenes one and two?

1

2

Use your stickers to place a paw print over each difference.

Phoenix's house

Phoenix lives in a very colourful house in Windsor Gardens. Use your stickers to add some more decorations.

Chakrabatics

Mr Brown has taken up 'Chakrabatics' to get fit, but he's not very good at it yet. Can you imagine what he's thinking about?

Draw a picture here.

A present for Aunt Lucy

Mr Gruber has an amazing pop-up book of London. Paddington thinks it will be the perfect present for Aunt Lucy's 100th birthday. Can you follow the right path to help him find it?

A B C D E

Get creative!

Paddington is very excited! There is a steam fair coming to town. Can you finish designing the poster?

MADAME KOZLOVA'S STEAM FAIR

Phoenix Buchanan is opening the steam fair. Can you spot five differences between scenes one and two?

①

②

Use your stickers to place a paw print over each difference.

Find the hidden sandwiches!

Paddington is working in a barber's shop to earn money to buy Aunt Lucy's birthday present. He has hidden five marmalade sandwiches around the shop in case of emergencies.

FRAGRANCES

MANICURES

EST. 1845

Can you spot them all?

A new look

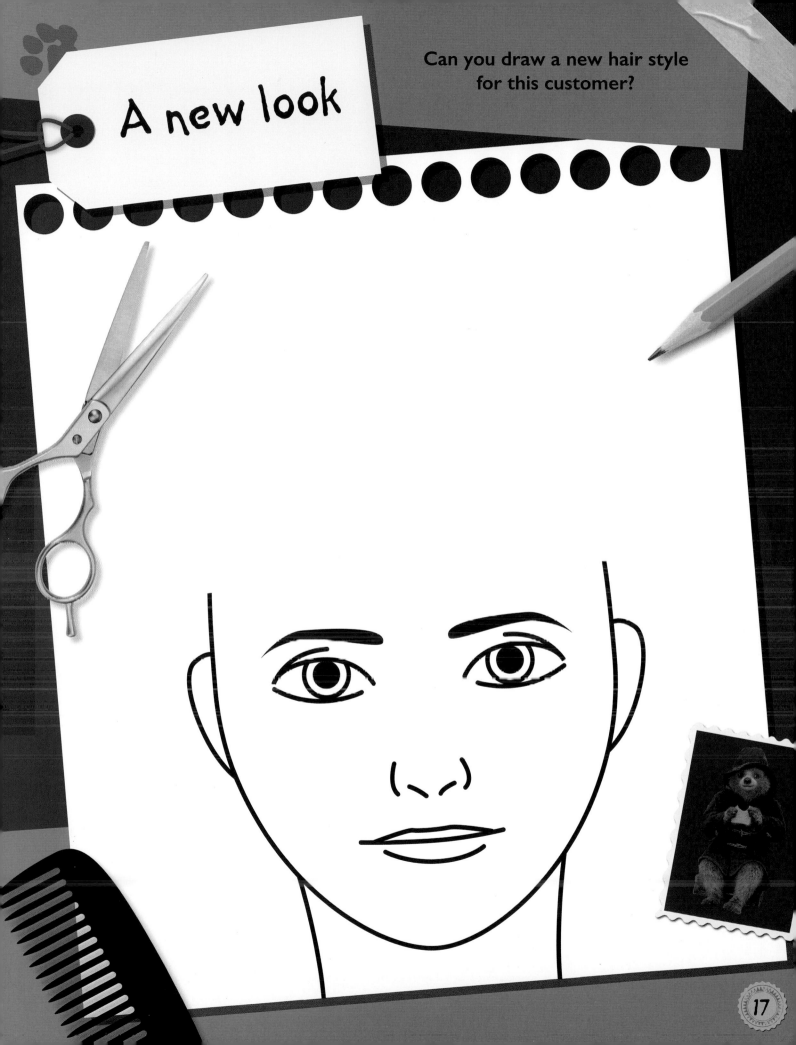

17

Snack time

Cleaning windows has made Paddington hungry. Can you copy the picture of him eating a marmalade sandwich into the grid below?

Dot-to-dot

GRUBER'S
•ANTIQUES•

OPEN

Join the dots to complete the picture of Paddington. Now colour in the scene.

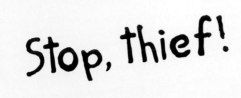
Stop, thief!

The pop-up book has been stolen from Mr Gruber's antique shop. Can you find the shadow that matches the thief's picture exactly? Place a paw sticker on the correct one.

A

B

C

D

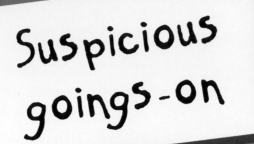

Suspicious goings-on

Paddington has been wrongly arrested for the theft of the pop-up book. Mr Curry has made a list of Paddington's 'suspicious activities'. Can you unscramble the words to complete the list?

Use your stickers to add the correct words below.

1. Taking a suspicious interest in Dr Jafri's YESK [   ].

2. Climbing up SDALERD [   ].

3. Looking through SWWODIN [   ].

4. Giving a customer a terrible IRAH [   ] cut.

5. Sneaking about in the AKRD [   ].

Paddington makes new friends!

Poor Paddington has been sent to prison because they think he has stolen the pop-up book. He misses the Browns but has made lots of new friends!

Knuckles

Spoon

Phibs

T-Bone

Charlie Rumble

24

Pages 2-3

Pages 4-5

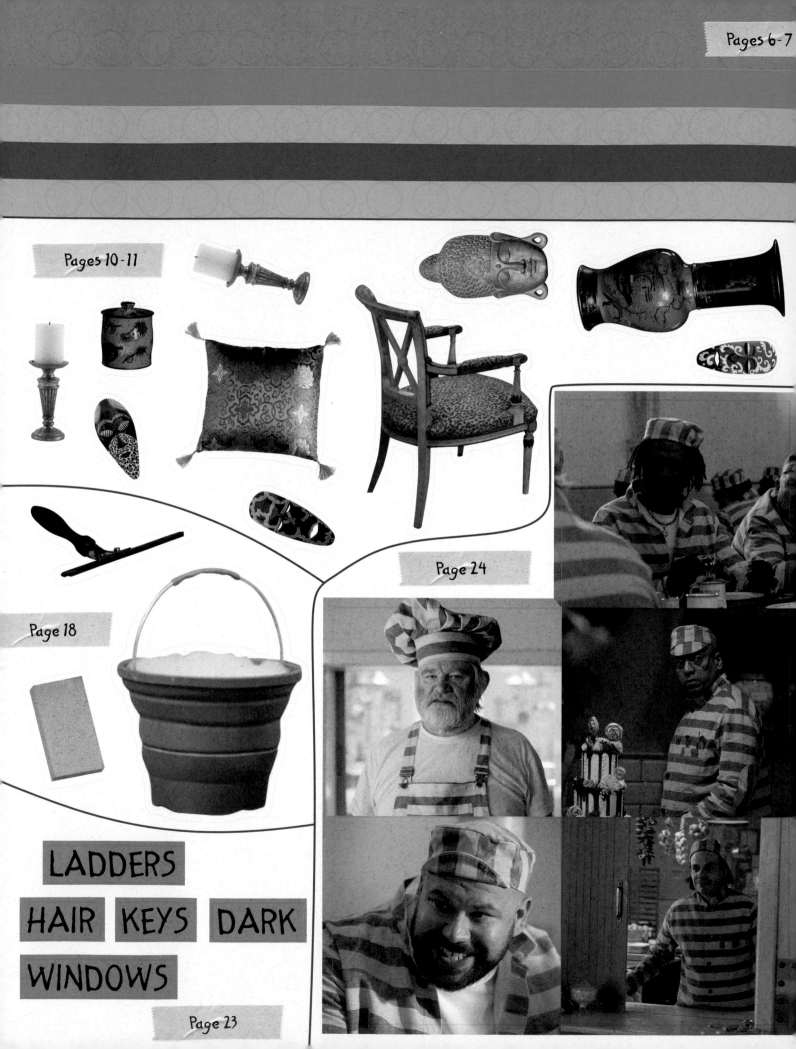

Pages 6-7

Pages 10-11

Page 18

Page 24

LADDERS
HAIR KEYS DARK
WINDOWS

Page 23

Page 26

Pages 28-29

Page 30

Page 31

smoke

disappearing

suspicious

stolen

Gruber's

Page 32

Pages 46-47

Page 34

Paw Stickers - Pages 9 & 15

Paddington's laundry mishap

Oops! Paddington accidentally dyed all the prisoners' uniforms pink. Can you design them a new one?

In the kitchen

Paddington is teaching Knuckles how to make marmalade. Use your stickers to add them both to the scene, and then find everything they will need to start cooking.

How to make the perfect marmalade sandwich

Paddington teaches his new friends how to make a delicious marmalade sandwich. Follow the steps below to make your own sandwich at home!

You will need:
★ A jar of marmalade
★ Two slices of bread
★ Butter or margarine
★ A plate
★ A knife (ask an adult to help you)

Instructions:

1. Take two slices of soft bread.

2. Carefully use a knife to butter each slice evenly.

3. Now spread plenty of delicious marmalade on one piece of bread.

4. Sandwich the two slices together.

5. Enjoy your delicious sandwich.

Yum! Yum!

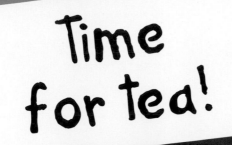

Time for tea!

Paddington has transformed the prison, thanks to Aunt Lucy's influence, and the prisoners have been busy baking! Can you get the canteen ready for afternoon tea?

AUNT LUCY'S RULES OF BEHAVIOUR

1. Always use a cake fork.
2. Never forget your manners.
3. Don't forget to raise your hat to strangers.
4. Never forget to write your thank you letters.
5. Always say please and thank you.
6. No shouting or being rowdy in public.
7. Don't rush, but always take your time.
8. Only complain with good reason when a hard stare is in order.

Use your stickers to add tea, cakes, buns and – of course – marmalade sandwiches!

Judy is printing newspapers to help to track down the real book thief. Use your stickers to complete the missing words.

HAVE YOU SEEN THIS MAN?

This [ ] character was spotted leaving [ ] Antiques the night that the pop-up book was [ ]. He was chased along the canal before [ ] in a puff of [ ]. The suspect had a shaggy beard and was wearing a hat.

HELP US FIND THIS MAN!

Now draw a picture of what you think the thief looks like.

Vanishing act!

Mrs Bird has been practising her disappearing tricks to help solve the mystery of the vanishing thief. Complete the jigsaw to make her reappear.

Who's the thief?

The story so far

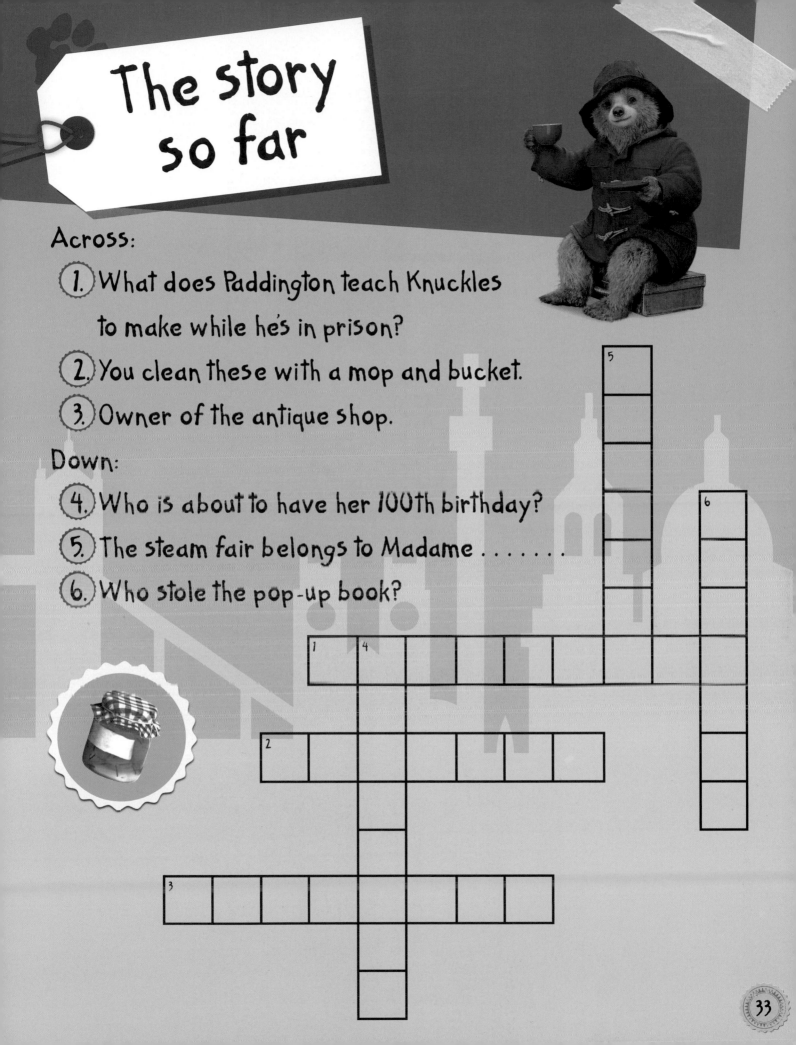

Across:

1. What does Paddington teach Knuckles to make while he's in prison?
2. You clean these with a mop and bucket.
3. Owner of the antique shop.

Down:

4. Who is about to have her 100th birthday?
5. The steam fair belongs to Madame . . . .
6. Who stole the pop-up book?

A dastardly disguise

Phoenix has been looking for Madame Kozlova's treasure all over London.

Can you use your stickers to give him two different disguises to wear while he searches for it?

Now draw yourself in disguise.

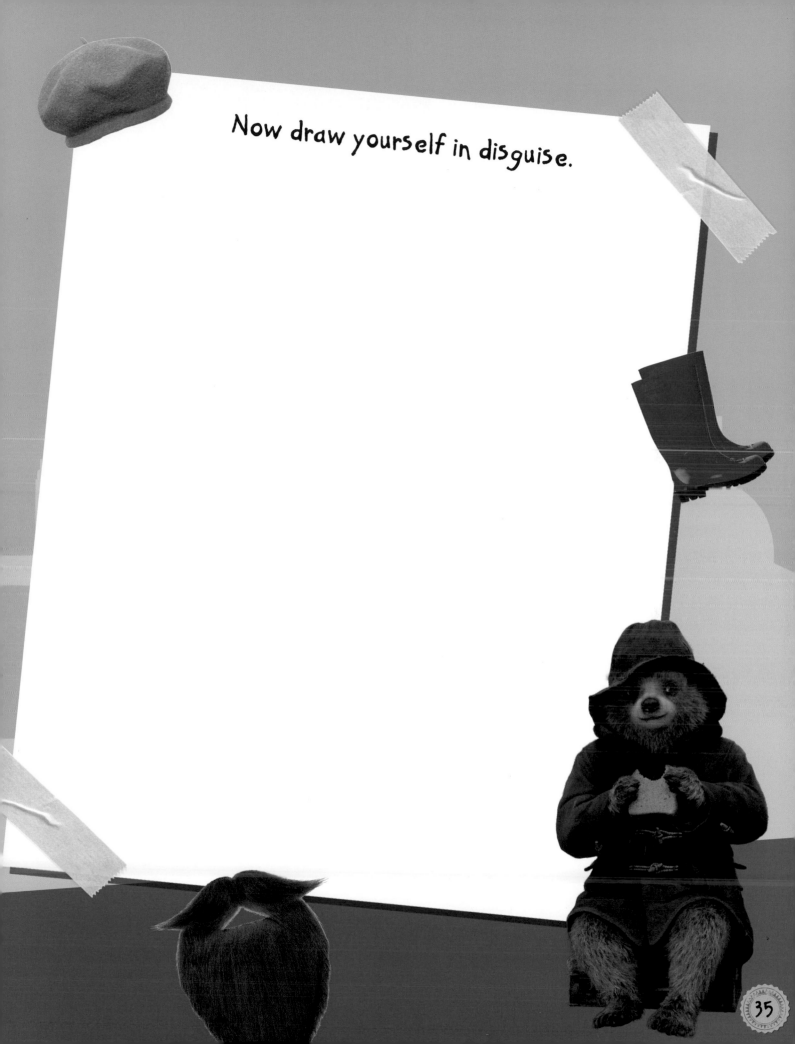

Catch Phoenix!

Mrs Brown is following the strange goings-on across London as she tries to track down the thief. Can you help her catch Phoenix?

You will need:

★ A die

★ Counters (You will find these at the back of your book).

How to play:

★ Take turns to roll the die. Whoever gets the highest number goes first.

★ Roll the die and move the number of spaces shown.

★ Follow the instructions on the squares.

★ The first person to catch up with Phoenix is the winner!

1 Start

2

3

4 You're stopped by a guard at Tower Bridge. Miss a go.

5

6

7

8 A friendly policeman gives you directions. Go forward one.

9

10

11

12

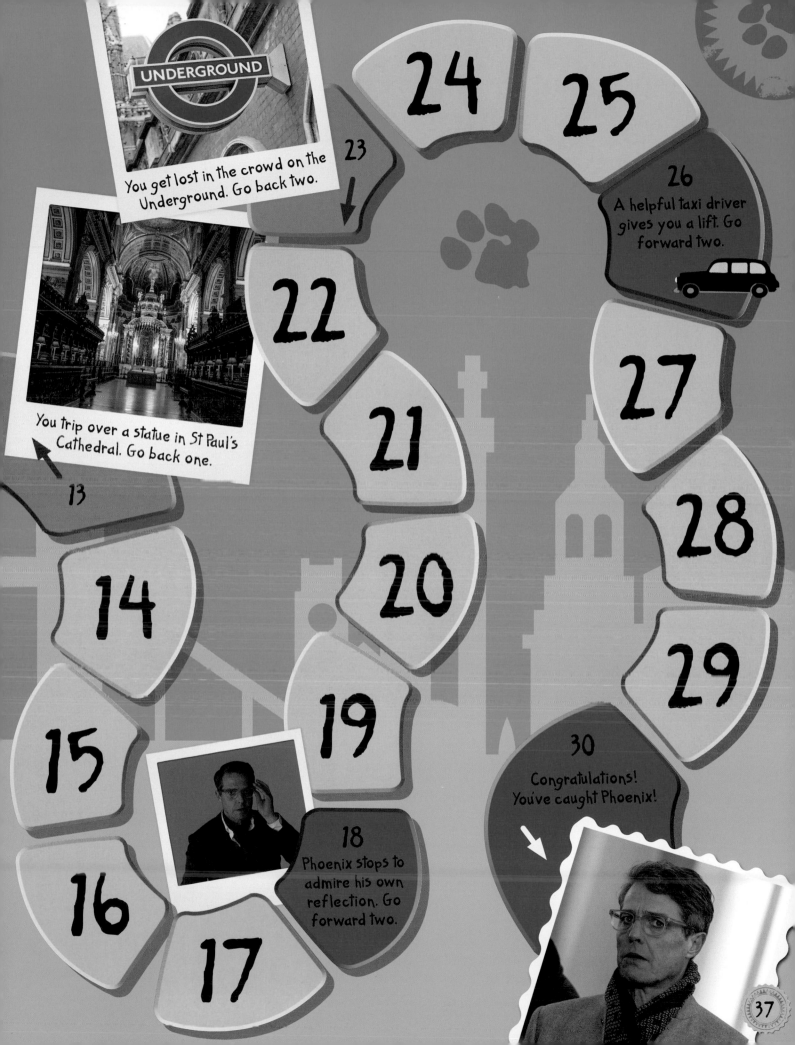

UNDERGROUND

You get lost in the crowd on the Underground. Go back two.

You trip over a statue in St Paul's Cathedral. Go back one.

13

14

15

16

17

18
Phoenix stops to admire his own reflection. Go forward two.

19

20

21

22

23

24

25

26
A helpful taxi driver gives you a lift. Go forward two.

27

28

29

30
Congratulations! You've caught Phoenix!

Help bring our bear home!

The Browns are campaigning for Paddington's release from prison. Can you help them by designing a poster?

FREE PADDINGTON

Please help us bring our bear HOME

Crack the code!

Use the alphabet along the top row to find the correct code letter underneath.

Key:

A	B	C	D	E	F	G	H	I	J	K	L	M	N	O	P	Q	R	S	T	U	V	W	X	Y	Z
Z	Y	X	W	V	U	T	S	R	Q	P	O	N	M	L	K	J	I	H	G	F	E	D	C	B	A

Code:

VHXZKV RM Z SLG

ZRI YZOLLM

_ _ _ _ _ _   _ _   _   _ _ _

_ _ _   _ _ _ _ _ _ _

39

Prison break!

Help Paddington and his friends to escape from prison and clear his name!

Start

2

3

4
You trip over pots and pans in the kitchen. Miss a go.

20 **19**

18
You find a shortcut through a trap door. Go forward two.

17 **16**

21

23
The escape route through the laundry chute is blocked. Go back two.

22

24 **25**

26
A guard has forgotten to lock the door. Go forward two.

How to play:

★ Take turns to roll the die. Whoever gets the highest number goes first.
★ Roll the die and move the number of spaces shown.
★ Follow the instructions on the squares.
★ The first person to escape is the winner!

You will need:

★ A die
★ Counters (You will find these at the back of your book).

Zzzz

5

6

7

8
You sneak past a sleeping guard. Go forward one.

9

10

15

14

13
You slip on a marmalade sandwich. Go back one.

12

11

Well done!
You've escaped!

27

28

29

30
Finish →

41

Welcome home Paddington!

Hooray! Paddington is home. Help welcome him back with this celebratory bunting.

You will need:

★ Scissors

★ Colouring pencils or felt tip pens

★ Glue

★ A piece of string

Instructions:

1. Carefully cut out the bunting, following the red dotted lines.

2. Use colouring pencils or felt tip pens to decorate the bunting on one side.

3. Place your decorated bunting with the blank sides facing up.

4. Place the piece of string along the centre of the shapes, lining it up with the green dotted lines.

5. For each piece of bunting, fold along the green dotted line and glue the folded sides together.

6. When the glue has dried, your bunting is ready to hang up!

Top tip: To make extra bunting use some blank paper to trace over the bunting before you cut it out.

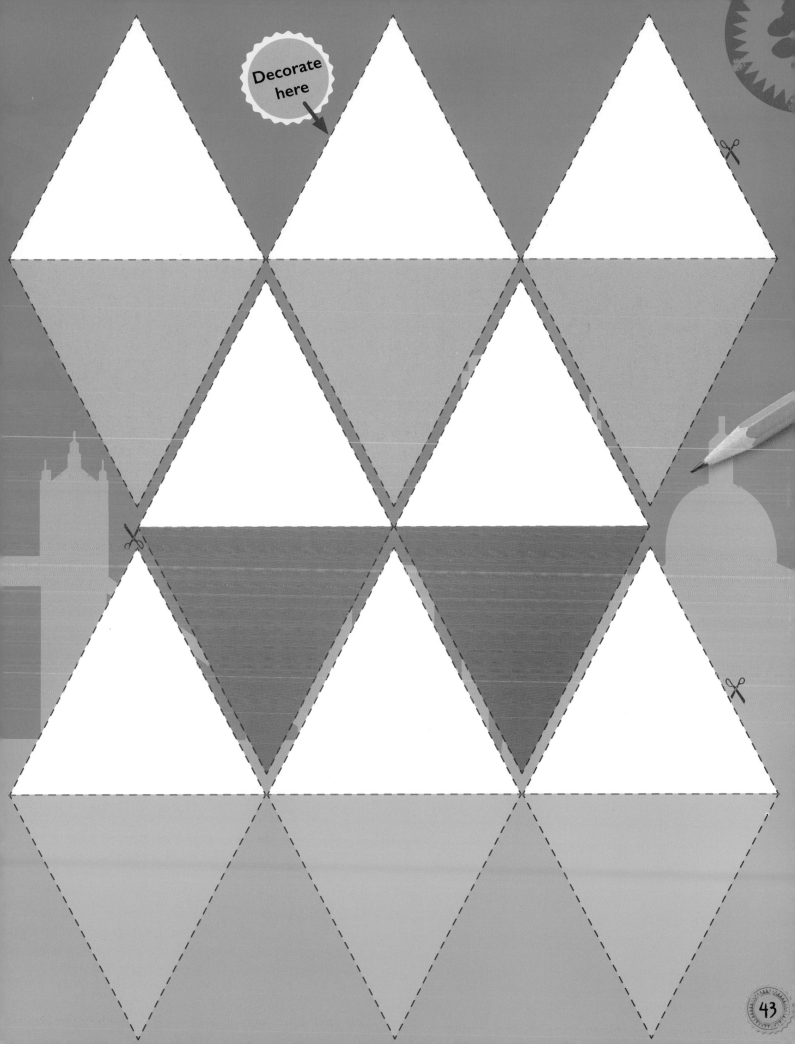

Decorate here

43

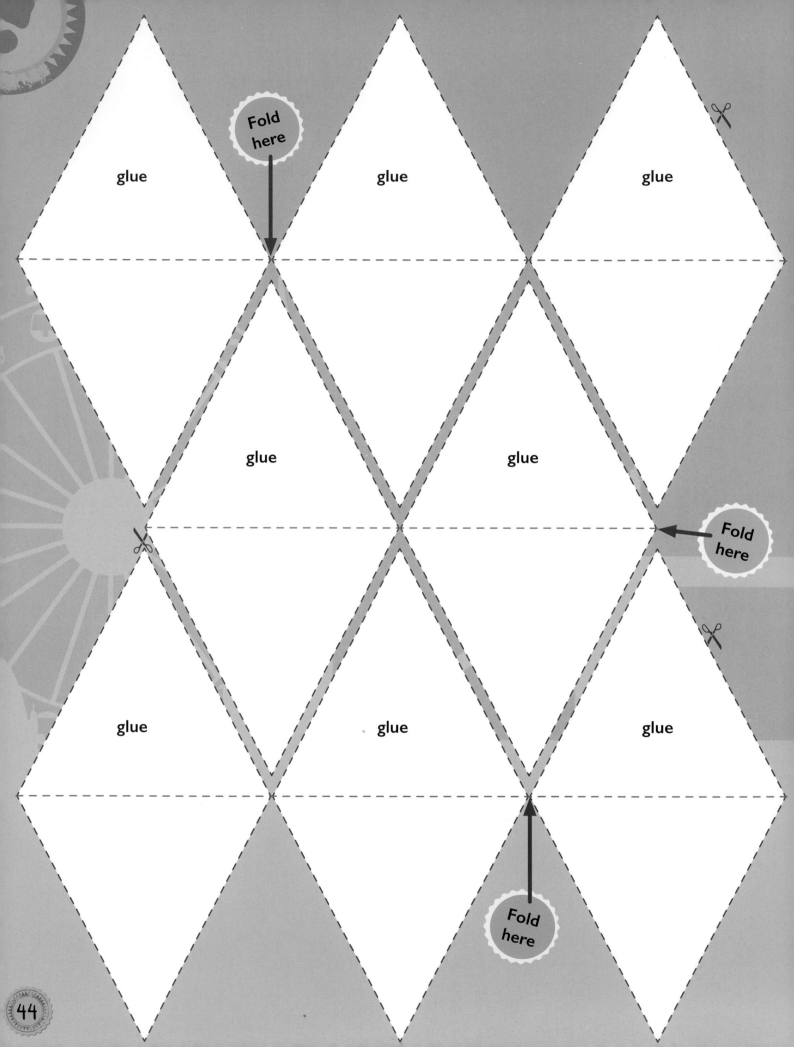

glue

glue

glue

Fold here

glue

glue

Fold here

glue

glue

glue

Fold here

44

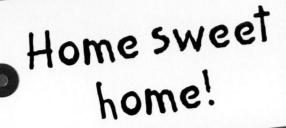

Home sweet home!

Paddington is so happy to see his friends again. Can you find their names in this wordsearch puzzle?

Jonathan Mrs Brown

Judy   Mrs Kitts

Mrs Bird   Mr Gruber

Mr Brown Dr Jafri

They can run down or across!

J	O	N	A	T	H	A	N	Z	J
M	R	G	R	U	B	E	R	I	S
A	H	Y	U	M	G	D	O	X	K
D	K	M	M	R	S	B	I	R	D
R	P	R	X	B	K	L	Q	U	D
J	A	S	C	R	O	P	R	Y	O
A	M	K	W	O	T	O	S	M	Z
F	P	I	L	W	X	C	M	Q	X
R	Y	T	H	N	C	N	E	T	S
I	D	T	T	L	M	U	F	J	N
B	E	S	M	P	O	G	L	U	P
X	N	I	S	J	N	Z	Q	D	L
N	O	L	F	O	E	O	U	Y	B
P	M	R	S	B	R	O	W	N	E

A very special guest

Everyone is incredibly excited to welcome Paddington back home. There is even a very special visitor from Darkest Peru!

Use your stickers to add Aunt Lucy to the scene.

47

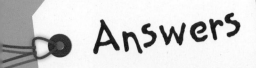

Answers

Page 8: Find the keys!

Start

Finish

Page 9: Nosy neighbour

Page 13: A present for Aunt Lucy

Path D leads to the pop-up book.

Page 15: Spot the difference!

Page 16: Find the hidden sandwiches!

Page 22: Stop, thief!

C is the correct shadow.

Page 23: Suspicious goings-on

1. Taking a suspicious interest in Dr Jafri's KEYS.

2. Climbing up LADDERS.

3. Looking through WINDOWS.

4. Giving a customer a terrible HAIR cut.

5. Sneaking out in the DARK .

Page 24: Paddington makes new friends!

Knuckles

Spoon

Phibs

T.Bone

Charlie Rumble

Page 30: Where's the thief

This suspicious character was spotted leaving Gruber's Antiques the night that the pop-up book was stolen . He was chased along the canal before disappearing in a puff of smoke . The suspect had a shaggy beard and was wearing a hat.

Page 31: Vanishing act!

Page 32: Who's the thief?

It was Phoenix Buchanan!

Page 33: The story so far

Page 39: Crack the code!

Escape in a hot air balloon.

Page 45: Home sweet home!

J	O	N	A	T	H	A	N	Z	J
M	R	G	R	U	B	E	R	I	S
A	H	Y	U	M	G	D	O	X	K
D	K	M	M	R	S	B	I	R	D
R	P	R	X	B	K	L	Q	U	D
J	A	S	C	R	O	P	R	Y	O
A	M	K	W	O	T	O	S	M	Z
F	P	I	L	W	X	C	M	Q	X
R	Y	T	H	N	C	N	E	T	S
I	D	T	T	L	M	U	F	J	N
B	E	S	M	P	O	G	L	U	P
X	N	I	S	J	N	Z	Q	D	L
N	O	L	F	O	E	O	U	Y	B
P	M	R	S	B	R	O	W	N	E

Door hanger

Make your very own
Paddington door hanger
for your room!

PADDiNGTON 2

Please come in!

Cut around
the dotted
lines
carefully.

Now hang it on your bedroom door!

PADDINGTON™ 2

BEAR 🐾 AT WORK!

Please come back later.
THANK YOU!

Make your own disguise!

Phoenix's attic is full of dastardly disguises. Follow the instructions to make your own mask.

1. Cut around the mask, following the dotted lines.

2. Carefully cut out two eye holes.

3. Decorate your mask with crayons, felt tips or paint. You could even add glitter!

4. Carefully make holes at the sides of the mask. Thread a piece of elastic through the holes and knot at both ends to secure it.

Counters

Cut carefully around the dotted lines to make your counters for the games on pages 36 and 40.

Be careful with scissors. Ask an adult to help you.

Mask

Counters

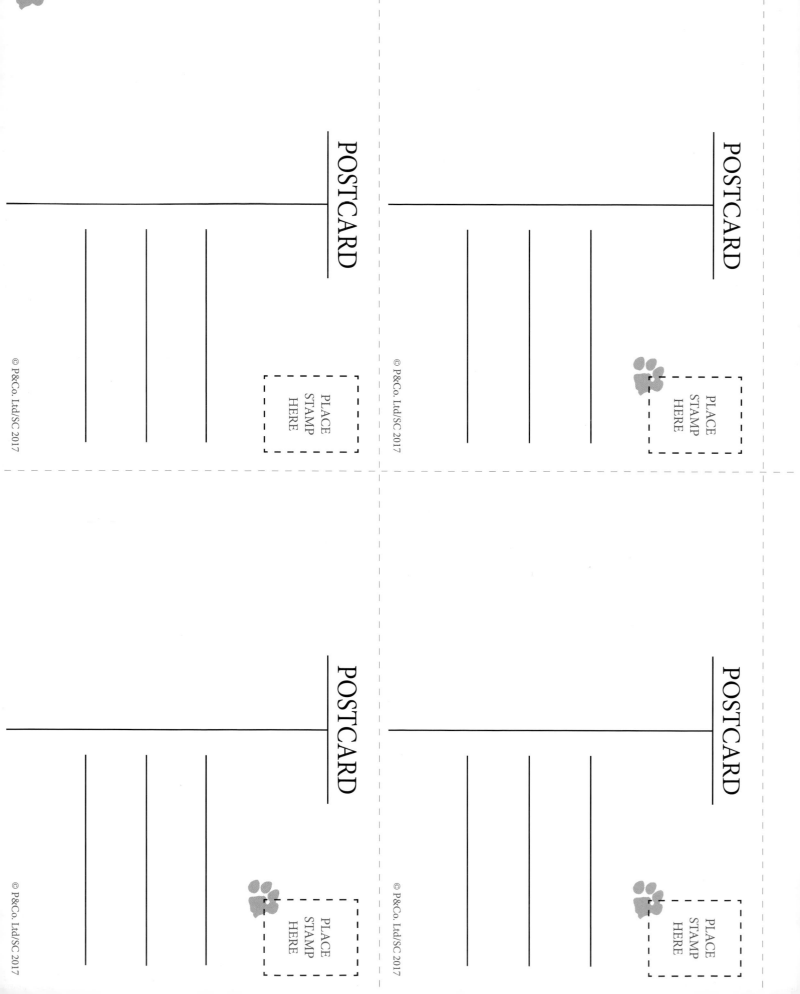

POSTCARD

PLACE
STAMP
HERE

© P&Co. Ltd/SC 2017

POSTCARD

PLACE
STAMP
HERE

© P&Co. Ltd/SC 2017

POSTCARD

PLACE
STAMP
HERE

© P&Co. Ltd/SC 2017

POSTCARD

PLACE
STAMP
HERE

© P&Co. Ltd/SC 2017

Marmalade sandwiches are useful for emergencies

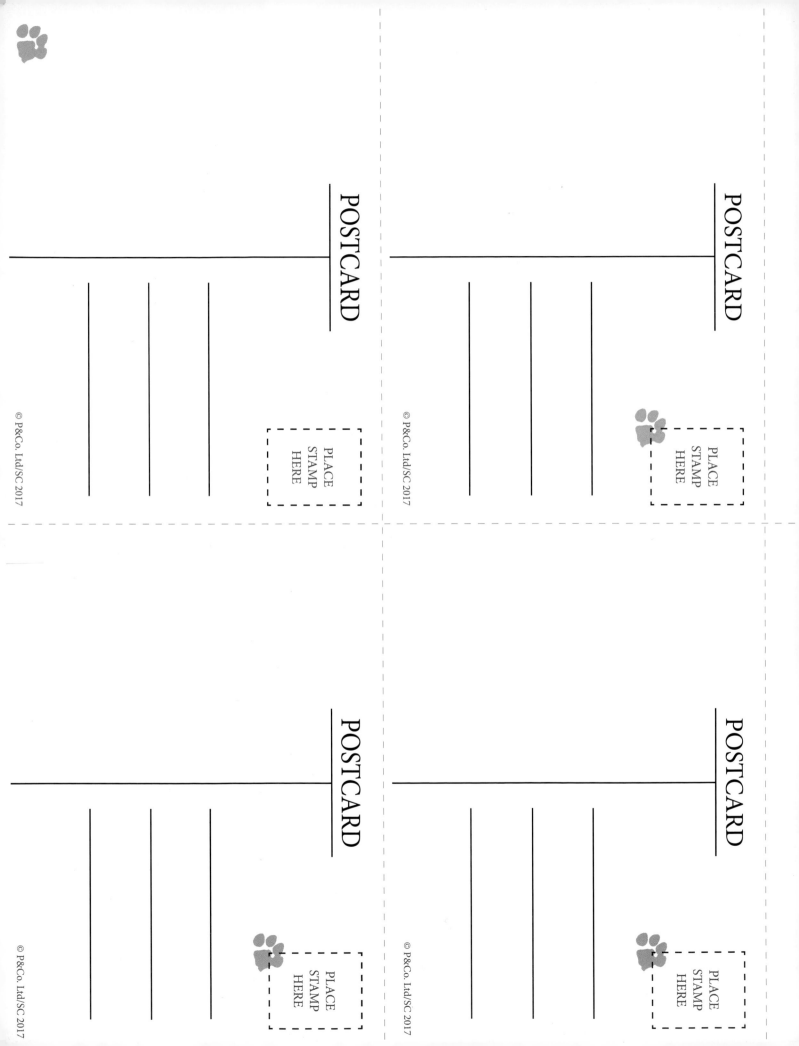

POSTCARD

PLACE
STAMP
HERE

© P&Co. Ltd/SC 2017

POSTCARD

PLACE
STAMP
HERE

© P&Co. Ltd/SC 2017

POSTCARD

PLACE
STAMP
HERE

© P&Co. Ltd/SC 2017

POSTCARD

PLACE
STAMP
HERE

© P&Co. Ltd/SC 2017